LITTLE MISS NEAT
and the last leaf

Original concept by Roger Hargreaves
Illustrated and written by Adam Hargreaves

MR. MEN   LITTLE MISS

MR. MEN™ LITTLE MISS™ © THOIP (a Sanrio company)

Little Miss Neat and the last leaf © 1998 THOIP (a Sanrio company)
Printed and published under licence from Price Stern Sloan, Inc., Los Angeles.
This edition published in 2014 by Dean, an imprint of Egmont UK Limited,
The Yellow Building, 1 Nicholas Road, London W11 4AN

ISBN 978 0 6035 6779 7
54225/2
Printed in Great Britain

Little Miss Neat likes things to be neat.

Which is why she is called Little Miss Neat.

She likes things to be as neat as two new pins.

Which is why her cottage is called Two Pin Cottage.

One autumn day Little Miss Neat looked out of her window to admire her very neat garden.

As she looked, a leaf fell from the tree in the middle of her lawn.

"Oh goodness gracious!" she cried.
"What a mess!"

She rushed outside, picked up the leaf, went back indoors and put the leaf in her rubbish bin.

"That's better," she said to herself.

But when she looked out of the window again there was another leaf lying on her immaculate lawn.

Out she rushed again and picked up the leaf and put it in the bin.

And so it went on all day long.

Rushing backwards and forwards until it was too dark to see anything.

Poor Little Miss Neat was exhausted.

"I don't like autumn," she murmured to herself as she fell asleep.

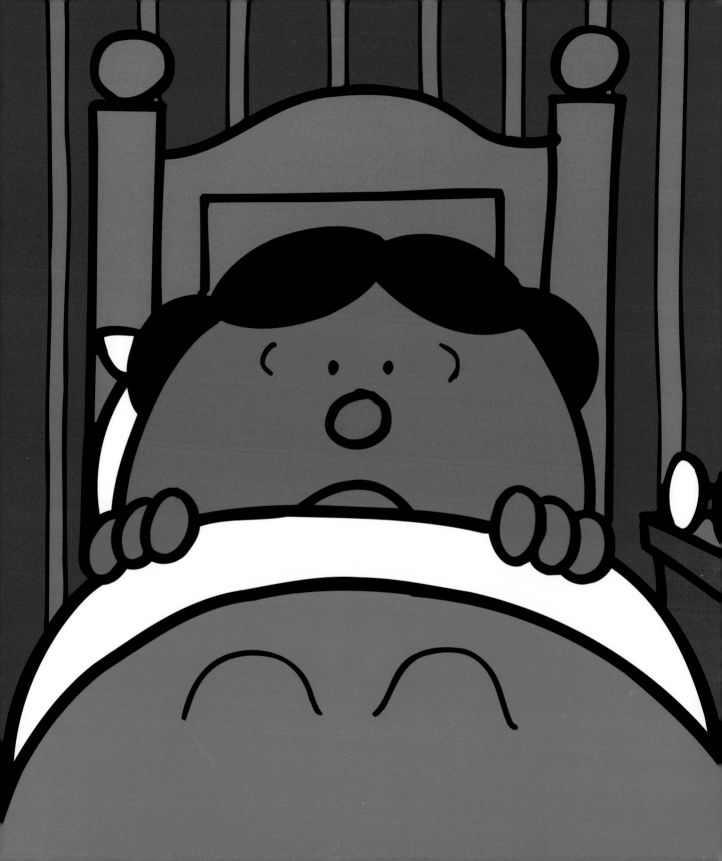

The next morning was even worse.

Little Miss Neat had to sprint to keep up with the falling leaves.

And that was how Mr Happy found her at lunchtime.

Running backwards and forwards.

"You look exhausted," said Mr Happy.

"I am," puffed Miss Neat, "but I have to pick up all these horrid, messy leaves."

"Do you know what I do?" said Mr Happy. "I wait until all the leaves have fallen and then I pick them up. You ought to try it. It's much easier."

After Mr Happy had left, Miss Neat thought about what he had said and decided she would try it.

But it was easier said than done.

Poor Little Miss Neat worried and fretted and fretted and worried as the leaves slowly covered her lawn.

She hated it.

But eventually all the leaves had fallen.

Well, nearly all the leaves.

There was just one leaf left on the tree.

Little Miss Neat waited.

And waited.

And waited.

When it got too dark to see she got a torch and waited.

And waited.

And waited.

All night long!

And that was how Mr Happy found her the next morning.

Still waiting!

"What are you doing?" asked Mr Happy.

"What you suggested I should do," replied Miss Neat. "I'm waiting for all the leaves to fall."

Mr Happy smiled, reached up and plucked the last leaf from the tree.

"Oh," said Miss Neat, suddenly feeling rather foolish.

And she blushed.

Mr Happy helped her to rake up all the leaves.

And by teatime Little Miss Neat's garden was as neat and as tidy as it usually was.

"You know what you should do next year?" said Mr Happy.

"Oh please! No more suggestions!" cried Miss Neat.

"Don't worry," said Mr Happy. "You'll like this one. I think that next year you should go on holiday and ask Mr Busy to clear up the leaves. It wouldn't take him a minute."

"What a good idea!" said Miss Neat.

"You've taken a leaf out of my book," smiled Mr Happy.

"And turned over a new leaf," chuckled Miss Neat.

"You can leaf through the holiday brochures," giggled Mr Happy.

"And I can leave the leaves behind," laughed Miss Neat.

"Hee hee, oh stop it, hee hee hee," laughed Mr Happy.

"Leaf me alone! Ha! Ha! Ha!"